Oh Look, It's A Nosserus

by
Kate Noble

Illustrations
by
Rachel Bass

Silver
Seahorse
Press

ISBN 0-9631798-2-9

First Edition
Manufactured in the United States of America
1   2   3   4   5   6   7   8   9   10

For Noble Bob
with love from Kate

To Jim
with love from Rachel

Robbi was a young rhinoceros

who lived in a park in Africa. Most

of the time Dilly, a white bird, rode on

his back. She ate the bugs that landed

on him, and she was fun to talk to. Today

she said she was going to fly for awhile,

just to keep in practice. So she was gone

when Robbi's big adventure began.

He heard the girl clearly. "Oh

look," she shouted, "It's a Nosserus."

Robbi didn't see very well, but

he knew it was a girl. The voice was

sweet and high, and she had flying

brown hair.

He ran away to the

pool where his mother was resting

in the mud.

"Mama, Mama, a Nosserus

is coming."

"A Nosserus? What's that?"

Robbi was shocked. "Don't you know?"

"No. Where did you see it?"

"I didn't. The girl did and

she shouted. I wasn't really afraid.

but I thought you'd want to know."

Mama lifted her beautiful horn. "Why

don't you ask Gerald if he sees anything?"

Robbi ran to the tree where Gerald

was eating lunch. Gerald looked down.

"How are you, Robbi?"

"Worried. A dangerous Nosserus is coming.

Can you see it?"

"Mm. I don't see anything dangerous. How do

you know it's coming?"

"The people saw it. They like dangerous animals."

"Yes, but they like us too," he nodded at his herd,

"and we're not dangerous. They like you, and you're

not dangerous, not when you look where you're going."

Robbi laughed. Gerald liked to

tease him about being clumsy.

''We have to find out if anyone

has seen the Nosserus,'' Robbi said.

He set off through the grass. The zebras would know.

They went close to the camp where the people stayed.

Joe Z and his sister Jessica were

chasing each other around in circles.

"Joe Z," Robbi called, "do you know

what a Nosserus looks like?"

"A Nosserus? What's that?"

"It's a dangerous animal and it's

coming this way. We need to find

out what it looks like."

Jessica tossed her head. "Everyone

knows what a Nosserus looks like," she said.

"He's bright red, like blood. And he has

three horns, jagged horns. He runs like

the wind." She caught her breath. "And

his tail. He has a sharp tail, like a knife.

But worst of all, he eats animals, any kind."

Robbi's eyes grew round. "What will

we do?"

"Warn everyone. Joe Z will help you."

"I will," Joe Z said.

They set off to spread the tale of the terrible Nosserus.

"It's huge," Robbi said.

"It has four jagged horns," Joe Z said.

"It's red as blood and has purple feet," Robbi said.

"Its tail is ten feet long

and sharp as a carving knife,"

Joe Z said.

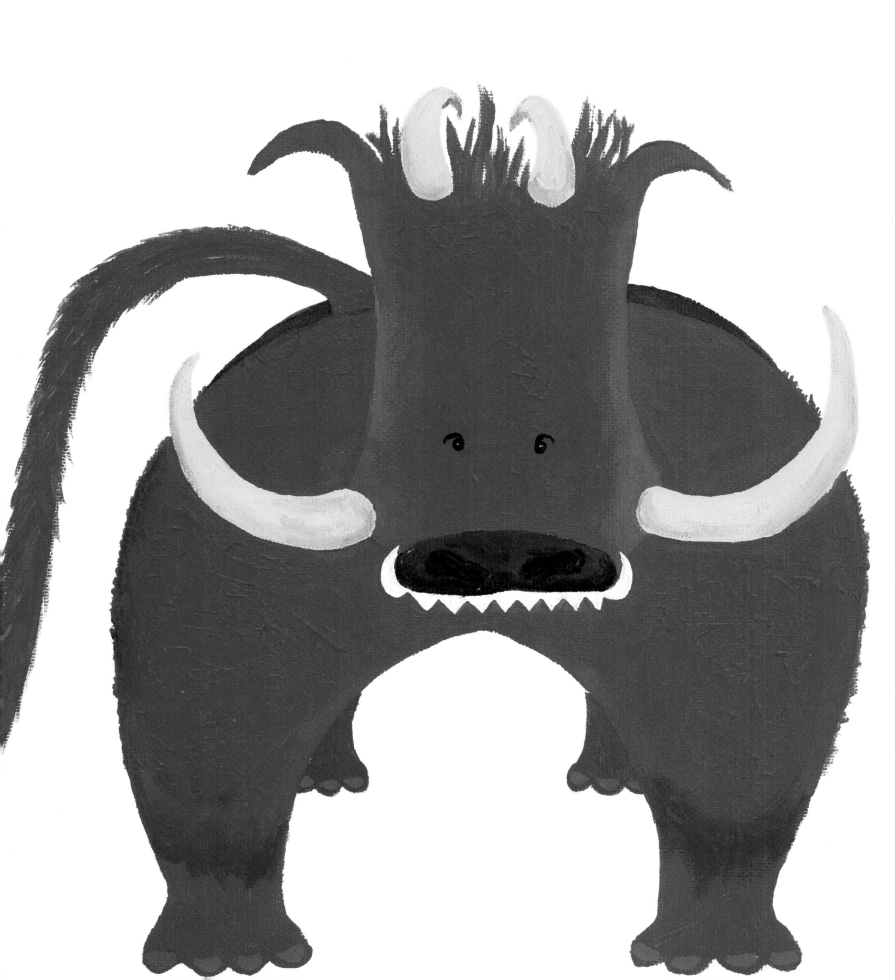

"It can eat an elephant," Robbi said.

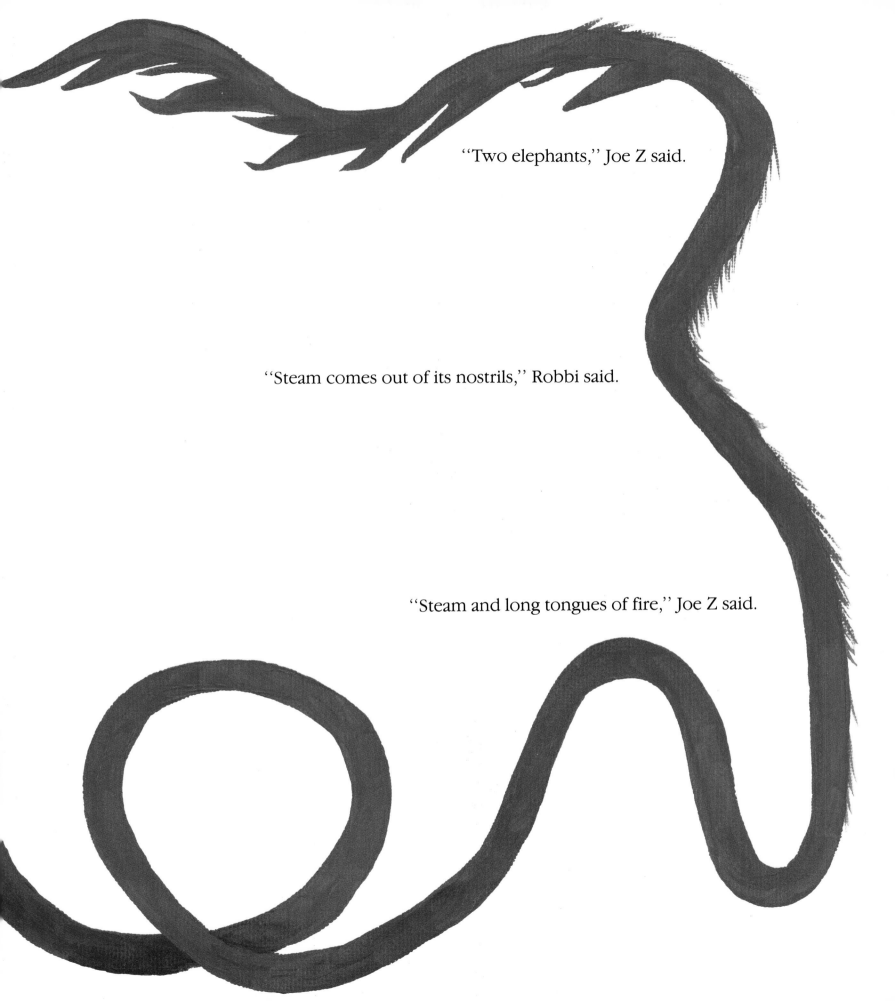

"Two elephants," Joe Z said.

"Steam comes out of its nostrils," Robbi said.

"Steam and long tongues of fire," Joe Z said.

When they had warned everyone,

an exhausted Robbi said goodbye to Joe Z

and went to find Mama.

Dilly was back from flying.

"Hi Robbi," she said. "Why were you running so fast?"

"I had to tell the animals about the Nosserus."

"The what?" Dilly hopped onto his back.

"The Nosserus. It's a dangerous beast, and it's coming.

I had to warn everyone."

Dilly smiled. "How do you know it's coming?"

"A girl said it. She shouted, 'Oh look, it's a Nosserus.'"

Dilly laughed.

"What's funny about a dangerous beast?"

"Oh Robbi," she said, "you're funny. Don't you see? You're the Nosserus."

"I am?"

"Yes. You're a Rhinoceros. She was looking at you."

"At me? But she shouted. I thought she was afraid."

"Well, look at you. You're a

very handsome, dangerous-looking

Nosserus."

Robbi laughed.

Dilly laughed.

Mama laughed.

"Hang on, Dilly," he said. "I have

to tell everyone. I have to warn them."

So he shouted as he ran,

"Oh look, I'm a Nosserus."